ReadZone Books Limited

50 Godfrey Avenue
Twickenham
TW2 7PF
www.ReadZoneBooks.com
© in this edition 2014 ReadZone Books Limited

This print edition published in cooperation with Fiction Express, who first published this title in weekly instalments as an interactive e-book.

Fiction Express
First Floor Office, 2 College Street,
Ludlow, Shropshire SY8 1AN
www.fictionexpress.co.uk

Find out more about Fiction Express on pages 61–62.

Design: Laura Durman & Keith Williams
Cover Image: Shutterstock Images
Printed in Spain by Edelvives

© in the text 2014 Sharon Gosling
The moral right of the author has been asserted.

ISBN 978-1-783-22469-2

REMY BRUNEL

BRUNEL

and the Circus Horse

Sharon Gosling

What do other readers think?

Here are some comments left on the Fiction Express blog about this book:

"The book is amazing."
Erin, Winchester

"This book is brilliant... really, really good :D"
Josh Price, Shrewsbury

"I can't wait to read the next chapter! I am all over the place I can't wait!"
**Ellie Millington Marsh,
Ludlow Junior School**

"I really like the story, it is really exciting ;D"
Holly M, Telford

"I was sad when I got to the end, I want to read more!"
Callum Crowther, Shropshire

Contents

*Many thanks to Laura and Paul
for their help and support.*

Chapter 1

The Circus Comes to Town

Constance the elephant was bored with waiting. She stamped her feet and puffed through her trunk as Rémy, sitting on her back, tried to keep her still.

"Not long now," the girl murmured into one of the animal's giant ears. "We'll be off soon, I promise. Be good and I'll find you an apple later."

Constance huffed and stamped some more.

Up ahead, the little town of Saint-Géry shimmered like an oasis in the sharp sun of morning. There were brightly-coloured streamers and flags of the French Tricolor hanging everywhere. There were posters, too, on every wall and even on the giant double doors of the town hall. *The circus is coming!* they said, *The circus is coming! Get ready to be amazed! Prepare to be astonished! Roll up, roll up, and see 'Le Cirque De La Lune' – the greatest show on Earth!*

The whole town had come out to see the circus arrive. The townsfolk knew that there would be jugglers and acrobats, lion-tamers and fire-eaters, as well as exotic beasts from the four corners of the world. No one wanted to miss the great procession. So there they all were, lining the streets, laughing and clapping, waiting for the dazzling show to begin.

Apart from when she was on the tightrope, practising her tricks, this was the bit of being part of a circus that Rémy liked the best. Today, she and Constance would lead the circus procession, right through the middle of town.

"Rémy Brunel! Are you ready?" Gustave the circus master called, from where he stood on the ground in front of the elephant. Dressed in his scarlet tailcoat, his polished gold buttons caught the sunlight and flashed as if they were on fire. On his head he wore a black top hat. In his hand he carried a whip, which Rémy knew could make a crack as loud as thunder.

"Yes, Monsieur Gustave," she called back. "We're ready."

"Then let's get this show on the road!"

There was a cheer from the circus folk, who were all dressed in their costumes for the procession. Rémy's favourites were undoubtedly the trick riders. These women all had purple leotards, studded with gold and shining stones like diamonds. They, and their horses, wore huge matching feather headdresses.

Rémy nudged Constance forward and the elephant lumbered after Gustave, her trunk high in the air, as excited as the rest of them. The crowds saw them coming and cheered as the circus band began to play, trumpets blaring and drums banging.

Looking over her shoulder, Rémy saw the acrobats turning cartwheels and leaping as they went. The fire-eaters lit their torches and blew great tongues of flame into the air. The lions roared as the lion-tamer stood on top of their open-sided cage and roared back. Behind all the performers were the brightly-painted wooden circus caravans. Their colours glinted in the sunlight, and the big horses that pulled them trotted happily amid the commotion.

The townsfolk loved it all. Rémy smiled and waved, and then surprised everyone by leaping to her feet and pirouetting like a dancer. She performed backflips, right there on Constance's back as the elephant continued to walk.

Glancing down, Rémy saw a boy of about her age running alongside them. Dressed in shabby clothes, he was looking up at the elephant in wonder. The road was uneven, and he wasn't watching where he was going.

"Look out!" Rémy called, "You're going to—"

It was too late. The boy's foot dipped into a pothole and he tripped, sprawling headfirst in the dust. The crowd laughed and pointed.

Constance stopped. Reaching down with her trunk, she picked him up and set him on his feet again. He was covered in dry dirt from the road, and so the elephant sucked in a trunkful of air and blew at him, dusting him off with one big puff.

"Th-thank you!" spluttered the boy. His hair stood up in all directions like a dirty dishmop, but he grinned happily as the crowd cheered. Then, sticking his hand in his pocket, the boy pulled out half a raisin bun and offered it to Constance.

Rémy grinned. "Go on, girl. You can have it. But be quick! You're holding us all up! The show must go on, you know!"

The elephant didn't need telling twice. Constance snatched up the bun, shoving it into her mouth. The crowd laughed and cheered again. Rémy turned to smile and wave at the boy. He waved back, a grin on his thin, dirty face.

Chapter 2

An Unexpected Visitor

Once the procession was over, the circus folk turned off into a field just outside the town. Then the real work began. Everyone changed out of their show clothes and pitched in to help put up the Big Top. Even Rémy had something to do – once the tent was in place, it was her job to polish the wooden benches that the strong men had carried inside.

She was just finishing up when she spotted the boy from the parade – the one who had given the bun to Constance. He was crouched in the shadows behind one of the stands, peering out.

"Hey," she said. "What are you doing here?"

The boy jumped and scrambled to his feet

with scared eyes. "I – I just wanted to see the elephant again," he stuttered.

"You're not supposed to be here," Rémy said, trying to sound stern. "The circus isn't open to the public yet."

"Sorry," said the boy, glumly. "I'll go."

"No, wait," said Rémy, catching his arm before he could leave. "What's your name?"

"Matthias. What's yours?"

"I'm Rémy," she said. "It was nice of you to give Constance that bun. She loves treats."

Matthias grinned. "Well, I love elephants. I can't believe that you're allowed to ride her. It must be amazing, living in a circus," he added, wistfully. "I wish I did."

Rémy looked him up and down. Matthias looked even dirtier and scruffier up close. His hair was still a mess, and his ragged trousers were caked with grime. His face was pinched and thin, but his eyes were kind, if a bit sad.

"Why don't you come and eat dinner with us?" Rémy asked. "We're having fish stew, and Tante Marie always makes too much."

"Won't she mind?" Matthias asked.

Rémy shook her head. "She likes feeding people. It's why she looks after me!"

"Doesn't she look after you because she's your aunt?" Matthias asked.

"She's not really my aunt," Rémy confessed. "But I've called her '*Tante*' since… since my mum and dad died."

"I'm an orphan, too," said the boy.

"So who looks after you?" Rémy asked him.

Matthias looked at his feet and dug one toe into the ground. "No one really."

"Well then," Rémy decided. "Tante Marie *definitely* won't mind you joining us for dinner."

* * *

Tante Marie welcomed Matthias the way she did everyone – with a bear hug and a huge kiss on both cheeks. Rémy grinned at the boy's slightly dazed expression. They sat down at the table and, as if by magic, huge bowls of stew appeared in front of them. It tasted delicious, and they both ate as if they'd never eaten before.

"So," said Rémy, between mouthfuls. "Where do you live, if you're all alone?"

"I found an old barn in the forest, not far from here," Matthias told her. "Nobody ever uses it. It's got holes in the roof and I have to

share with squirrels, but it's OK. At least it's...
somewhere."

"Will you show me?" Rémy asked.

"What, now?" Matthias looked doubtful.

"Why not?"

"It'll be dark soon," Matthias reasoned. "And
anyway, I haven't seen Constance. Or the lions!
Can I see the lions?"

Tante Marie bustled back in from the caravan's
tiny kitchen. "Are you full, chicks?" she asked,
"Because if you are, hurry along and leave me
to read the tea leaves. Young Claudette wants
a lesson. You've got at least an hour to play
before the sun goes down. Rémy could show
you the new tightrope tricks she's been learning,
Matthias. Be back before dark, mind. Oh, and
watch out for those... those new arrivals."

"What new arrivals?" Rémy asked with a
frown.

"Two brothers – magicians. They've just
arrived and they're parked over by Gustave's
caravan." Tante Marie shook her head.

"Don't you like them?" Rémy asked.

"I haven't met them yet, Rémy. They may be
fine folk. But...." she paused, and Rémy knew
she was hiding something.

"What?" she asked. "Tante Marie? Did you see something in the tea leaves? What was it?"

Tante Marie smiled and shrugged. "I saw trouble, that's all. Maybe it's nothing, but it was just as those two arrived. So stay away from them, *d'accord*? Go and see the animals, but come back before it gets dark."

Outside, the circus was quiet. Everyone was inside, eating dinner. The animal enclosures stood behind the Big Top, away from the caravans.

"Constance has her own tent," said Rémy, pointing to it. "Let's go and see her first. I bet she'll remember you."

"Really?" Matthias asked, surprised.

"Haven't you ever heard the saying, 'An elephant never forgets'?"

"Yes, but I didn't think it was true!"

"Well, it is," said Rémy, as they passed the lion cage. "I bet she'll take one look at you, and–" She stopped.

"What's wrong?" Matthias asked.

"Look!" Rémy whispered, her voice scared. "The door to one of the lion cages is open!"

It was, too. The metal bars creaked slightly as it swung in the evening breeze.

"Rémy, I can't see the lion," said Matthias, suddenly very scared.

Rémy was breathing fast. "Me neither," she said. "And—"

There was a noise behind them. They both spun around. There was something inside the Big Top. It was slinking against the wall, casting a shadow that leapt against the canvas.

"What do we do?" Matthias asked, petrified.

Chapter 3

Big Trouble

The shadow continued to slink along the wall of the Big Top. Matthias wanted to run, but his legs wouldn't move. He could feel his heart beating extra hard, crashing against his ribcage as if it were trying to escape.

"Let's go back to the caravan," Rémy whispered, her eyes fixed on the shadow. "Very slowly and very quietly, we'll–"

There came a sudden sound from behind them. Something grabbed Matthias by the shoulder, hard. He yelled in fright as he was spun around to face a horrible-looking man. His head was bald apart from stubbly bits of hair sticking out above his ears. He had a big, hooked nose, hollow cheeks and angry eyes that stared out from beneath dark, bushy eyebrows, and he was dressed all in black.

"I know what you're up to," he shouted, right in Matthias's face. Turning towards Rémy, he pointed at the open lion cage. "This was you, wasn't it? The two of you kids, playing a foolish prank!"

Matthias struggled, but couldn't get away from the man's grip.

"Let him go!" Rémy screamed, running forward and kicking the man's shin.

He cursed and tried to grab at her, but Rémy dodged out of the way, too quick for him. "Tante Marie!" she shouted, "Gustave! Anyone! Help! Help!"

There came the sound of running and Tante Marie appeared, followed by Gustave the circus master. Gustave, so fat that he was always out of breath, looked as if he might explode at any moment. His cheeks were bright red with the effort of running.

"What is it?" Gustave wheezed, "Have you seen the lion?"

"This man grabbed us!" Rémy shouted. "Make him let Matthias go!"

"They're responsible," said the stranger, still

holding on to Matthias. "They were playing a game, the way stupid children do, and let the lion free."

"That's a lie!" cried Rémy.

"We didn't do anything!" Matthias protested, still struggling. His shoulder was really hurting. "We were just going to see Constance!"

Gustave turned to the man. "Did you actually *see* them set the lion free?"

"Well," said the man, shrugging. "That is to say, I...."

"This is nonsense!" said Tante Marie, her voice full of scorn. She shooed the man away, standing between him and the children. "Gustave, Rémy knows better than to open any of the animal cages. Who is this stranger, anyway?"

The horrible man squared his shoulders. He was very thin and extremely tall. He towered over Tante Marie. "I am Arturus Augusto. My brother Alberto and I are the magicians of this circus. And I am telling you that if there's trouble, there's bound to be children in the middle of it. These two were up to no good."

"And I'm telling you...." Tante Marie began, angrily.

"Enough!" barked Gustave. "We have more

important matters to attend to. Arturus and his brother came highly recommended, Marie. They're part of this circus now... unlike *this* young man," he said, glaring at Matthias.

Rémy made as if to say something, but Tante Marie got there first.

"Matthias is a cousin who lives in the village," she said, quickly. "He came to visit, that's all."

Gustave nodded, but his scowl remained. "You know there should be no outsiders at the circus before it opens."

"Yes Gustave, I'm so–"

Her apology was interrupted by a great shout. It echoed from the other end of the circus field.

"We've found him!" someone yelled. "QUICK, we've got the lion cornered – HELP!"

Gustave hurried away. The magician sneered angrily at the children before following in his wake.

Tante Marie took Rémy and Matthias back to her caravan, locking the door as she left again.

* * *

"Are you all right?" Rémy asked Matthias as he rubbed his sore shoulder.

Matthias nodded. "Yeah. But that man – Arturus…." he shuddered.

"I know," Rémy agreed. "He's creepy." She looked around, and then cleared Tante Marie's fortune-telling teacup away and began to drag the dinner table across the caravan floor.

"What are you doing?" Matthias asked, puzzled.

Rémy pointed to the caravan's ceiling. There was a small hatch in it, with a handle. "We can climb up on to the roof and watch what's going on," she explained.

Matthias hesitated. "Won't we get into more trouble?"

"Of course not," she said. "Why would we? And we didn't do anything wrong in the first place, remember?" Rémy pushed open the hatch and, a moment later, disappeared from view. Matthias heard her moving about on the roof. Then she stuck her head back inside. "Well, come on!" she said. "What are you waiting for?"

Chapter 4

Noises in the Night

Matthias hesitated for another moment, and then scrambled after Rémy. Outside, the sun was setting. The caravans were casting shadows that marched along the ground like an army, growing longer and longer by the minute. Soon they would all join together and night would fall completely.

"There, look," said Rémy, pointing to a large ring of circus people standing in a semi-circle near one of the fences. Most of them were holding big sticks. "That must be where the lion is."

"They won't hurt it, will they?" Matthias asked, wondering about the sticks.

"*Non,*" Rémy told him. "They'll just guide

him back to his cage and try not to get bitten along the way."

Matthias looked around, taking in the view. Something caught his eye at the circus entrance. "Hey," he said. "There's the magician. What's he doing?"

Rémy turned to look. Arturus was leaving. He had draped a long, black cloak around himself. As the children watched, he pulled a big hood up over his head. Checking over his shoulder to make sure he hadn't been seen, he slipped out of the circus field's gate. He headed into the thick forest that surrounded it, disappearing in the gathering darkness.

Rémy stood up. "Quick," she said, "Let's follow him!"

"What?" Matthias asked, startled, as she headed for the side of the caravan and began to climb down. "We can't!"

"Why not? Don't you want to know what he's up to, going into the forest this late at night?"

"Well, yes, but... but... Tante Marie told us to stay in the caravan!"

"No, she didn't," called Rémy. Matthias looked over the edge of the caravan to see her gripping on to the side, as nimble as a spider.

In another moment she was on the ground, looking up at him. "She didn't tell us to stay in the caravan. She just locked us in. And she's actually been teaching me how to pick locks. So when you think about it, it could have just been a test…. So come on! If you're too scared, I'll go without you."

"But it's almost dark!"

"*D'accord*," she said, turning to walk away. "I'll be back before you know it."

"All right, all right," Matthias grumbled. He lowered himself from the roof of the caravan, reaching to secure a foothold on one of the large wooden wheels. But as he loosened his fingers, his foot slipped and he landed in a heap on the ground.

Rémy reached out a hand to help him up. "I'll have to teach you how to climb," she said, smiling. "I've been having lessons as part of my tightrope training. I can go really high now," she told him. "Right. Let's go."

They dodged through the shadows to the gate, as quiet as mice. The dark forest loomed ahead, as if ready to swallow them up.

"Do you really want to go in there?" Matthias asked, anxiously.

Rémy shrugged, but he could tell she was nervous. "I want to know what Arturus is up to. There's no reason to be afraid. You live in the forest, don't you?"

"Er, yes," said Matthias, nervously. "But I don't usually go out after dark."

"Why not?" Rémy asked, staring at him with big eyes.

He made a face, feeling the hair at the back of his neck prickle a little bit, as if an icy wind had suddenly brushed over it. "Some people say there are wolves and... and *ghosts* in there."

Rémy didn't say anything for a moment. Then she took a deep breath. "Come on," she said. "If we stay together, we'll be fine."

But they had only gone a little way into the darkened forest when they heard a terrible sound. It burst over them with the evening wind, a high-pitched whinnying that was so loud and so awful that they both covered their ears. The noise rose and fell, starting and stopping.

Rémy and Matthias froze to the spot, scared by the sound.

"What is it?" Matthias asked, clutching Rémy's arm.

She shook her head, pretending not to be afraid but not really succeeding. "I don't know. It doesn't sound like a person.... Maybe we should just come back tomorrow–"

"Wait!" whispered Matthias, as the haunting noise echoed through the trees again. He pointed. "Look!"

Chapter 5

Mystery in the Forest

Matthias was pointing into the darkest depths of the wood. Through the trees floated a mass of shimmering white.

That horrible noise sounded again as the weird shape lurched from side to side, dipping and weaving jerkily.

"I told you!" said Matthias, clenching his hands so hard that his fists turned white. "There are ghosts in this forest!"

Rémy hadn't ever seen a ghost before, and she was pretty certain she wasn't looking at one right now, either. It definitely wasn't the ghost of a person, she decided – it was too big, for a start. And there was no sign of the form having arms or a head, either.

Matthias scrambled to his feet. "Come on," he said, his voice shaking. "You were right. Let's get out of here!"

He turned to head back the way they had come, but Rémy stopped him, pulling him down behind a tree. "No," she hissed. "Let's hide and see what happens."

The apparition was now so close that they could feel the ground shudder beneath them as it moved towards their hiding place. It was still weaving from side to side. Each time it did, there was a grunt, as if someone was trying to pull something that really didn't want to move.

Rémy could hear branches snapping beneath what sounded distinctly like heavy footsteps, too. It was clear that the mysterious creature, whatever it may be, was certainly not a ghost. Still, she squashed closer to the tree's trunk to make sure she was not seen as it passed.

There was a tiny 'clink' as something flew through the air and hit the tree, just above their heads. Falling to the ground, it plonked into the soft mulch beneath a bush, millimetres from Rémy's left foot.

The 'ghost' crashed on through the forest. Its bellows grew quieter as it moved away, until, after a few moments, they both breathed a sigh of relief.

"I can't believe how close that was!" hissed Matthias. "You nearly got us caught by a ghost!"

"It wasn't a ghost, Matthias!" Rémy told him, impatiently. "The ground shook as it went past. Ghosts can't do that!"

"Can't they?" Matthias said, doubtfully. "I–"

"And," Rémy continued, interrupting him as she pulled the object from beneath the bush, "how many ghosts do you know that can throw one of these?"

Matthias stared at what she was holding up. It caught the light of the moon and shone silver in the darkness.

"It's a horseshoe!" he exclaimed, taking it and turning it around in his hands. "Where did that come from?"

"From a horse, I expect," said Rémy, cheekily. "Come on, let's follow it."

Matthias stood up, brushing old dry leaves from his trousers. "Follow it? Follow what?"

Rémy sighed. "The horse, of course! The one that just went past us covered in a sheet."

Matthias followed her, confused. "That… that was a *horse*? But – but the awful noise!

I've never heard a horse make that kind of sound before!"

"Neither have I," admitted Rémy, "It was obviously really scared. Creatures make all sorts of noises when they're frightened. And it was clearly being dragged along by something... or someone. Hurry up, or we'll lose it!"

Chapter 6

Rémy to the Rescue

They ran after the ghostly form of the covered horse, which was still weaving through the forest far ahead.

"It's trying to get away," Rémy hissed, over her shoulder. "That's why it keeps dipping and jerking. Poor thing."

"But who – or what – is it trying to get away from?" Matthias asked, looking down as he tried not to get caught in the tangle of tree roots under their feet.

"That's what we're going to find out!" Rémy declared. Then she stopped. "Wait – where did it go?"

Matthias stopped beside her. Rémy was right. The ghost – or the horse, if Rémy was right –

had disappeared. They could no longer see it floating through the trees ahead of them, and the forest had closed around them in deathly silence. Suddenly a dim yellow glow bloomed somewhere ahead. It was so faint that if there had been any more light from the moon, they wouldn't have seen it at all.

"I know where we are!" whispered Matthias, a flash of recognition striking him. "That's my barn – the one where I sleep! Someone's found my candles and lit one. That glow is shining through the hole in the roof!"

"This barn," said Rémy, "is it big enough for a horse, by any chance?"

"Yes, of course," said Matthias. "That must have been what it was used for at one point, I suppose. Or cows, maybe. Not any more, though."

"Alright then. Lead the way. Let's find out what's going on."

Matthias stepped forward. Now that he knew where they were, the forest seemed a less scary place, and he could make his way through it much more easily. He and Rémy crept towards the small clearing that surrounded his home.

The barn was larger than Rémy had imagined,

and about as ramshackle as it could possibly
be. The wooden planks that made up its high
walls had swollen and warped in the rains of
many years. Some had even popped out entirely.
Others had crumbled away like rotten teeth,
leaving gaps for the wind to whistle through.
Part of the roof had fallen in, too.

Matthias and Rémy dropped to their knees
and crawled closer to peer through one of the
broken planks. Inside they could see a horse
tethered firmly to a branch that poked through
the barn's wall. The animal was no longer
covered by a sheet, and they could see that it was
brown, apart from one dash of white on its right
hind leg. It was shaking its head, still scared and
showing the whites of its eyes as it fidgeted.

"Stay still, you little—"

Matthias and Rémy both jumped at the angry
sound of the man's voice. They hadn't even
noticed him standing with his back to them –
a tall man in a black cloak.

Rémy grabbed Matthias' arm and silently
mouthed, "Arturus!"

But when the man turned, they saw that it
wasn't the magician after all. It was another man,
someone they'd never seen before. He had pale

cheeks and angry eyes beneath a mop of lank, greasy brown hair. In one hand he was carrying a big can of white paint, and in the other he held a large paintbrush. As they watched, he dipped the brush into the paint and then slapped it on to the horse's hide! It whinnied and shied away.

"I told you to keep still!" growled the man. "It's only a bit of paint, you stupid animal!"

He carried on daubing paint on to the poor horse until, instead of being pure brown, it looked like a skewbald pony – similar to the carthorses that pulled the circus caravans. Then he put the paint down and left the shack.

"I'll bet that was Alberto," hissed Matthias. "You know, Arturus's brother."

Rémy clutched the boy's arm. "I'm sure you're right," she whispered, urgently, "but we can't leave the poor horse like that. We've got to wash the paint off before it dries!" She began to crawl forwards through the gap.

"Wait!" he whispered back. "The man might only be gone a minute!"

"I'll be quick," she insisted. "You stay here – keep watch!"

Before Matthias could stop her, she had scrambled through the gap and was standing inside the barn. She looked around briefly before crouching down to speak to him again. "Where do you keep your water?"

"There's a bucket I use for washing – beside the bed. But–"

She was gone before he had a chance to say anything else.

Going to Matthias' makeshift camp bed, Rémy grabbed the bucket, sloshing some of the water over the side. She picked up a rag from the floor, too, and went over to the horse, talking to it gently to calm it down. Rémy dipped the cloth in the bucket and began to rub at the paint. The horse stood still, quivering but calm.

"YOU!" An angry shout sounded from the door of the barn.

This time, it *was* Arturus, the magician!

Rémy dropped the bucket of water and the horse reared. One of its hooves knocked over the lighted candle. It skittered across the floor, before nestling into the thick covering of old, dry leaves. They all caught fire in a trice. In seconds, the flames were out of control. The horse gave a terrified whinny, desperate to get away, but it was still tethered to the branch.

"Rémy!" Matthias yelled. "Get out! Run!"

Chapter 7

Caught in the Blaze

Matthias knelt in the gap, horrified to see the flames growing by the second. The smoke they gave off billowed thick and black, filling his nose and lungs.

Arturus leapt forward, grabbing at the scared horse. He tried to pull it out of the door, but the animal was tied fast. He let go again.

"We have to leave!" he shouted to Rémy, over the roar of the flames.

"We can't just abandon her!" said Rémy.

"It's just a horse!" the magician shouted. "Don't be stupid, girl!"

Ignoring him, Rémy wrestled with the thick rope, but she couldn't loosen it.

"Fine," Arturus yelled. "Suit yourself!" He ran,

disappearing through the growing smoke and out into the dark forest.

Matthias shouted through the gap. "Please, Rémy," he called. "You've got to get out – now! Come on!"

Rémy took no notice. The flames crackled and spat as they continued their fearsome journey, devouring the dry old wood like an angry monster crunching at its prey.

Rémy pulled something from a pocket in her trousers. Matthias squinted, trying to make out what it was. It glinted in the light of the blaze, and he saw that it was a little penknife. She flicked open the blade and began sawing at the horse's tether, trying to free the terrified animal.

Matthias knew at once that it was useless. She'd never cut through the rope in time to escape the flames. As if the fire were agreeing with him, there was an almighty crack from overhead. Matthias looked up as the last full beam of the roof gave way under the fire's gnashing jaws. It crashed to the floor, sending sparks and tongues of flame shooting up into the air and blocking Rémy's main escape.

The horse screamed in terror and it reared again. The force snapped the weakened rope, freeing the animal but knocking Rémy to the ground. The horse wheeled, jumping clear over the burning roof-beam and dashing out into the forest.

"Rémy!" Matthias yelled, but she didn't get up. He could hardly see her through the thickening flames and smoke. If he didn't do something, she'd be burned alive!

Matthias ducked through the hole and into the barn. Inside, the heat was almost unbearable. He coughed, tried to breathe, and then coughed again as the thick scorching smoke filled his nose and lungs.

"Hey!" he shouted, dropping down beside Rémy. He shook her shoulder. "Wake up! You've got to wake up!"

There was a whooshing sound. The circle of flame surrounding them had almost closed. Another moment and they would be trapped for good.

Suddenly Rémy moved. She coughed, opening her eyes and then immediately screwing them up against the smoke. She sat up and put one hand to her head, looking around. In another second she was on her feet, swaying slightly.

"We have to climb," she shouted at Matthias,

pointing to the one wall that was still untouched by the flames. That part of the roof had fallen in years ago, so there was a ragged gap at the top. If they could somehow get up it and down the other side before the fire got there, they'd be safe.

"We can't get over that!" he shouted back. "It's too high, there's nothing to hold on to!"

"There's always something to hold on to!" Rémy ran to it. "Follow me – and don't look down. Don't think about it, just do it. *D'accord?*"

She didn't stop to see if he nodded. Instead, Rémy kicked off her shoes and threw herself at the wall. Almost immediately she was several feet off the ground, finding footholds anywhere she could – in narrow splits in the old wood or knots of tree that had fallen out over time.

Coughing and spluttering, Matthias followed. His throat felt hoarse and his eyes were so sore that he could hardly see. But he pushed himself up behind Rémy. She reached the top and turned to look down at him. For a moment, Matthias saw a flicker of worry in her eyes.

"What's wrong?" he yelled.

"Nothing," she said. "Keep going – don't look down. Just don't look down!"

He scrambled harder, but he was nowhere near as good a climber as Rémy. Matthias, panicked, jammed a toe into an open knot and began to haul himself up a few feet, but his foot slipped. He slammed against the wall, his knees scraping down the wood as his feet dangled helplessly.

He felt heat on his soles, and couldn't help looking down. The fire looked very, very close. Too close....

Something grabbed him by the wrists. It was Rémy. She'd hooked her legs over the edge of the wall and was stretching both arms down to him.

"I said, don't look down!" she yelled. "Now, for goodness' sake – *climb*!"

Chapter 8

A Shocking Discovery

With Rémy's help, Matthias made it to the top. The scramble down the other side was easier, although he lost his grip a few metres from the bottom and fell, sprawling on the thick forest floor below. He stared up, dazed, as flames licked over the wall they had just escaped, sending flickering smoke signals into the night sky.

"Get up," Rémy urged, breathless, pulling Matthias to his feet.

"We've got to get help," he spluttered, as they stumbled away. "We have to tell someone in Saint-Géry about the fire, before the whole forest catches alight!"

"Can you find your way in the dark?"

"I think so," gasped Matthias. He pointed to a wider path that led away from what had once been the front of the barn. "The road's just down there. Quickly!"

They ran, the crackle of the fire growing fainter behind them. When they reached the town, there was no sign of anyone. Rémy realized that most people would be tucked up in bed for the night.

"Where's the police station?" she asked, urgently. "That's where we should go."

"It'll be shut," said Matthias, "but I know where the policeman lives!"

Matthias led the way to a little grey brick house that stood beside the silent police station at one end of the village. They banged on the door until they heard footsteps. The door opened slowly, the policeman's sleepy face emerging from the gloom beyond. He wore a long, shabby nightgown and a nightcap was perched crookedly on his bald head.

"What's happening?" he asked, with a yawn. "What do you want at this time of night?"

"There's a fire!" the children said, together.

"In the forest," explained Matthias, "The old barn – it's going to burn the whole forest down if you don't do something! Look!" He pointed to the glow in the air hanging above the trees.

"*Mon Dieu*!" whispered the policeman, no longer sleepy. "We must wake the town!"

He disappeared back inside his house and Matthias breathed a sigh of relief. He turned to Rémy to say something, only to find her gone.

"Rémy?" he called. "Where are you?"

"Here," she said. She was standing outside the police station, in the light cast from the open door, staring at something on the wall. Matthias went over to look. It was a poster.

WANTED, it said, FOR ROBBERY.

Apparently, two men had held up a train carrying a lot of gold coins that had been bound for Paris.

"What?" Matthias asked, puzzled, as Rémy continued to stare at it. "Why are you–"

"Look," said Rémy, pointing.

Matthias leaned closer. It seemed that the police didn't have a description of the two men, who had been wearing masks – but they did have a description of the horse that had pulled their getaway cart. It was a mare, the poster said, black all over, except for a distinctive white splash on her right hind leg.

"That's why they were painting the horse," whispered Rémy. "It's them! The magicians are the robbers, and they had to disguise their getaway horse!"

Matthias frowned. "But the horse we saw was brown, not black," he said.

"It's a very dark brown!" Rémy insisted, "Perhaps they got the description wrong – it was night-time, so maybe the people on the train couldn't see exactly what colour the horse was. I'm certain it was them, Matthias. We have to investigate!"

"Oh no," said Matthias, taking a step back and holding up his hands, "hold on a minute–"

"Come on," Rémy insisted. "They're bad men, we know that already. And why else would they be trying to disguise the horse? I've got to tell Monsieur Gustave. If they're caught at the circus, the police will think we all had something to do with it!"

Footsteps sounded as the policeman made his way over to them. He was now wearing his uniform, although he'd dressed so quickly that his policeman's cap was askew. "Right, you two," he said. "What do you know about this fire, eh?"

Chapter 9

Last Try

Rémy and Matthias looked at each other. The policeman crossed his arms.

"Well?" he said. "I asked you a question."

"We just happened to be passing and saw the fire," Rémy replied, quickly. "So we came to warn you. That's all."

"Oh really?" said the policeman. "And what were you two youngsters doing out so late?"

"We just went for a walk," Matthias explained. "We didn't realize how late it was."

"Exactly! Er… which means we really should be getting back," added Rémy. "People will be worried about us. Come on, Matthias!"

"Hey – wait!" The policeman tried to catch Rémy, but she ducked under his arm. Running to the wall, she tore the 'wanted' poster from it before taking off down the path. Matthias followed after her.

"*Arrêtez!*" the policeman shouted, "Come back here!"

Rémy and Matthias sped back to the circus. By the time they got there, they were both out of breath and tired. They stumbled through the gate and headed straight for Gustave's caravan.

It was so late that most of the circus people had gone to sleep for the night. Rémy ducked into the dim, shadowy gaps between the darkened caravans.

Matthias followed, but the blackness suddenly made him nervous. Now that they'd stopped running, he was cold, and he kept imagining that things were lurking beneath each caravan they passed.

He froze as something caught his eye from behind the spokes of one of the wooden wheels. Two green eyes blinked at him slowly. He nearly laughed out loud – it was just one of the circus cats! Then he realized that Rémy was no longer in front of him.

"Rémy?" he whispered. "Where are you? Wait for me!"

"Stay back," she hissed, from the gloom ahead. "I don't want Gustave to see you!"

He stayed where he was, and spotted her disappearing around the corner of another caravan. She reached the wooden steps of Gustave's home and ran up them, the 'wanted' poster clutched beneath one arm.

Matthias watched as Rémy reached up to knock. Before she could, the door opened right in front of her, a burst of light silhouetting the person standing there.

But it wasn't Gustave – it was Arturus, the magician. He towered over Rémy, glowering at her. Matthias ducked behind the steps of the caravan opposite, careful to keep in the shadows.

"Where's Gustave?" Rémy demanded, angrily. "Let me speak to him!"

Arturus moved aside and the circus master appeared in the doorway. "Rémy," he said. "Now is not the time. I've been hearing some very bad things about you."

"Whatever he said," Rémy cried, jabbing a finger in the magician's direction, "he's lying! He and his brother, they're thieves. The police are looking for them. I can prove it!"

"Rémy, stop," said Gustave. "Go home. It's

past your bedtime. Let me talk to Arturus and I will listen to your side of things in the morning."

"Wait!" she gasped, unrolling the 'wanted' poster and holding it up to Gustave. "It's them – Arturus and Alberto – they're thieves. The police are looking for them! If they find them here, we'll all be in trouble!"

Gustave raised one eyebrow in disbelief.

"You have to believe me," pleaded Rémy. "I saw their horse – it had the white marking on its leg just like it says here. They were trying to disguise it. But then there was a fire and the horse ran away."

"Rubbish," scoffed Arturus as Gustave took the poster from Rémy. "I don't even have a black horse. Our pony is a skewbald mare." He looked at the circus master with a shrug and a little smile that made Rémy want to scream. "You know what children are like, Monsieur Gustave. They imagine all sorts of things."

"I am *not* imagining this!" cried Rémy.

"Well, let's go and find out, shall we?" Arturus sneered.

"Wh-what?" Rémy faltered, but Gustave and Arturus had already set off for the magicians' caravan.

Matthias followed, keeping to the shadows. Arturus was just too calm. And when they reached the spot where he and his brother had pitched their home, Matthias saw why.

"There, you see?" said Arturus, smoothly. "Our brown and white horse, all hitched up and ready to go."

Rémy was speechless. She stared at the pony standing calmly between the shafts of the magician's caravan. Then she recovered. "B-but, don't you see, Gustave? They've painted it. To disguise it."

"Oh, really?" asked Arturus, crossing his arms. "Yes!"

"So this horse supposedly escaped from a fire less than an hour ago?" Arturus looked at Gustave and rolled his eyes. "I'd imagine such a horse would still be pretty terrified, wouldn't you? This one seems rather too calm for that, I would say."

Rémy clamped her lips together to stop them trembling. The horse *was* calm, it was true. "It's… it's exhausted!" she cried. "And look how bloated she is Gustave. They don't even know how to feed and look after her properly!"

"Really, Rémy, that's enough!" Gustave sighed

heavily and turned to the magician. "I am sorry for the disturbance, Arturus," he said. "As you say, Rémy has an active imagination. We will leave you in peace now. Have a safe journey."

"Journey? What journey?" Rémy asked.

"Our mother has been taken seriously ill, back in Paris," said the magician, calmly. "My brother and I will not be able to stay with *Le Cirque de la Lune* after all. We are leaving tonight."

"No!" exclaimed Rémy. "Gustave, you can't let them go! They're lying! They're leaving because they know that Matthias and I have found out the truth!" She pointed at the pony. "This is the horse in the poster. We just need to wash it and you'll see! It's not really a skewbald at all – they're hiding it from the police. And the police will come here, looking for them, and if they're not here, *you* will be accused of helping them to escape! Let me get some water, Gustave, and I'll prove it!"

Arturus shook his head. "Gustave. I've gone along with this crazy charade long enough, don't you think?"

"Yes, I do," agreed Gustave. "Rémy, it's time for you to stop playing this silly game. Do you hear me?"

Rémy hung her head. Matthias, looked around, quickly. If he could just find a bucket of water, he could throw it at the horse right in front of Gustave's eyes. He saw one standing beside the steps of the caravan next to where he was hiding.

But before Matthias could reach the bucket, Arturus's evil brother Alberto clamped a hand over his mouth. He tried to kick himself free, but his captor held him fast. He struggled, bit, and tried to yell, but nothing did any good. Matthias watched as Gustave ordered Rémy home to her bed, said goodbye to Arturus, and disappeared into the shadows.

"I know what you are," he heard Rémy say, defiantly, "and I'll make sure you get caught."

"Is that so?" said Arturus, in a voice that hissed as surely as a snake's. "Well, we can't have that, can we?"

The magician lunged towards the girl and bundled her up the stairs before she even had a chance to scream. Matthias was next – he found himself carried into the caravan and dumped on the floor beside Rémy. They both tried to scramble up, but Arturus and his horrible brother were too strong.

"Tie them up, Alberto," Arturus ordered. "We've got to get out of here."

"What are we going to do with them?" asked Alberto, as he bound and gagged the two struggling children.

Matthias looked up at Arturus's cruel, sneering face. "We'll think of something," he whispered. Matthias shivered with fear.

Chapter 10

The Truth Will Out

The two men left the caravan and shut the door behind them. A moment later there was a shudder and it began to move. It juddered slowly over the uneven ground of the field, heading for the gate. The two captives tried to yell, but through the gags it was useless. There was no way they could make anyone hear.

Then Rémy remembered. Of course! She still had her penknife! She'd put it back in her pocket in the barn.

Rémy managed to shuffle around enough to nudge Matthias with her shoulder. She jerked her chin at her pocket. Fortunately, the boy got the message. With his hands tied it seemed to take him ages to get the penknife out and open.

The task was made even more difficult by the rocking of the wagon over the uneven field.

Matthias frowned, concentrating as he sawed frantically at the thin rope around Rémy's wrist.

Come on, come on, Rémy urged, silently. They had to get out before the wagon left the circus ground! A second later she felt the rope giving way. Rémy strained against it, pulling her sore hands in different directions until it split and she was free.

"Ugh!" she spluttered, pulling the gag out of her mouth and then reaching out to do the same for Matthias before releasing his hands.

Leaping up, they pulled and banged at the door, but it wouldn't open – the magicians had locked it.

Then a sound echoed to them from outside. It was one of the circus lions, roaring. They were passing the animal enclosure!

Matthias ran to one of the small windows. "Help!" he yelled, hoping that one of the keepers might hear. "Help! We're being kidnapped! Help! Someone, please help!"

Still no one answered, and the caravan didn't stop. Matthias yelled some more, but it was no good – there just weren't any people around to hear. Then there came another, louder sound. It punched the air like a huge firework, powerful, high-pitched and very, very angry. There was the sound of thumping, and the ground shook.

"It's Constance!" Matthias shouted. "The elephant! Hey! Constance! Over here! Hey!"

The thumping and trumpeting continued. Then there came other sounds – the sounds of the circus folk coming out of their homes to find out what all the fuss was about.

The caravan pulled to a stop.

"Get out of the way!" they heard Arturus shout, angrily. "Stupid animal, you're blocking the path! Move!"

Meanwhile, Matthias and Rémy banged their fists on the side of the caravan, until eventually, the door was flung open to reveal the chubby, puzzled face of Gustave.

"Rémy?" he asked, confused. "What are you doing in there?"

Rémy rushed out. "They tried to kidnap us!"

"Oh, don't be absurd," scoffed Arturus, as he appeared around the side of the caravan. "These children have been causing us trouble all week. They must have snuck inside to steal something and then got stuck!"

"That's a lie," Matthias said, really angry now. "They tied us up with these ropes!" He threw the ropes and gags at Arturus's feet. "You were taking us away because we know the truth. You're thieves, and we can prove it!" He jumped down the steps and ran to where Constance was being calmed by her keepers. As soon as she saw Matthias, she stopped stamping and reached out with her trunk to pat him on the head.

"Constance," he said. "Water. We need water!"

The elephant immediately stuck her trunk in a nearby barrel of water and sucked up every last drop.

"Constance," Matthias continued. "Spray… right there!" He pointed in the direction of the pony, which was still standing, tired and quiet, between the caravan's shafts. Constance didn't hesitate, spraying a jet of water right at the horse.

A silence fell over the assembled circus folk as they saw what was happening. The horse shivered and neighed, but stood still as all its white patches began to run and drip. Constance continued to spray until all of the white was gone and the horse was dark brown again – all except for one white splash on her right hind leg.

"Well," said Gustave, to Arturus and Alberto. "What have you two got to say to that, eh?"

But the magicians were silent.

The circus master turned to Rémy. "It seems you were right, little one," he said. "I should have listened to you."

Rémy beamed. She knew that this was as close to an apology as anyone would ever get from Monsieur Gustave.

* * *

The policeman did come, a few hours later, when the fire was out and most of the forest was safe. He took both of the magicians into custody, had a quiet chat with Gustave, and then searched the brothers' caravan. Inside, hidden in several old, battered biscuit tins, he found the gold coins stolen from the train.

Rémy and Matthias didn't care about the magicians. Rémy was too worried about the poor pony. Once it had been led away from the caravan, it lay down and refused to move. Rémy was so concerned that she asked the horse trainer to come and look at her.

"Well, Rémy," he said kindly, after taking one

look at the pony. "I can tell you she's going to be fine. She's just going to need a bit of help for the next few hours, until the foal arrives."

"Foal?" Rémy repeated, puzzled.

"Yes," said the trainer. She's about to have a baby, Rémy. Do you want to help me deliver it?"

"Oh, yes! And of course, that's why she was so calm after the fire!" Rémy realized. "She knew she was about to have her foal! Poor pony."

The foal, when it arrived, was a beautiful, pale palomino filly. Rémy helped her stand for the first time, her shaky little legs tottering all over the place.

"She's a pretty little thing, isn't she?" said a voice. Rémy turned to see Gustave, standing with his arms crossed, watching. "She needs a name, don't you think?"

"Dominique," Rémy said, patting the tiny horse gently. "I think we should call her Dominique."

"Why don't you leave Dominique for a moment, and come with me?" Gustave suggested. "I want your help with Matthias."

Rémy did as she was told, patting the pony one more time before following Gustave. "Why?" she asked. "What's he done this time?"

"Look," said the circus master, pointing. Outside, the night had broken and a pale pink dawn was beginning to creep over the horizon. Rémy followed Gustave's finger, and saw Matthias standing by Constance, rubbing her trunk. She kept patting his head. It looked very much as if they were having a conversation.

"I told him, Gustave – an elephant never forgets," said Rémy. "I think she likes him."

"I think so, too," the circus master agreed. "So I was wondering – do you think he'd like to join us and become part of the circus? He could train as one of Constance's keepers."

Rémy grinned. "Yes," she said. "Yes, I think he'd like that very much."

THE END

FICTION EXPRESS

THE READERS TAKE CONTROL!

Have you ever wanted to change the course of a plot, change a character's destiny, tell an author what to write next?

Well, now you can!

'Rémy Brunel and the Circus Horse' was originally written for the award-winning interactive e-book website Fiction Express.

Fiction Express e-books are published in gripping weekly episodes. At the end of each episode, readers are given voting options to decide where the plot goes next. They vote online and the winning vote is then conveyed to the author who writes the next episode, in real time, according to the readers' most popular choice.

www.fictionexpress.co.uk

FICTION EXPRESS

TALK TO THE AUTHORS

The Fiction Express website features a blog where readers can interact with the authors while they are writing. An exciting and unique opportunity!

FANTASTIC TEACHER RESOURCES

Each weekly Fiction Express episode comes with a PDF of teacher resources packed with ideas to extend the text.

"The teaching resources are fab and easily fill a whole week of literacy lessons!"
Rachel Humphries, teacher at Westacre Middle School

If you enjoyed this story, you might also like to read *The Mystery of Maddie Musgrove*. Here is a taster for you…

Chapter 1

An Amazing Discovery

Joe stared up in horror. A plane was falling out of the sky, trailing clouds of black smoke. It was heading straight towards him! Terrified, he turned and began to run through the graveyard. He ran so fast he lost his balance and tumbled, scratching his bare knees and banging his head on a gravestone.

Glancing behind, he saw the dark shape of the plane closing in on him, engine screaming, fire spurting from its wings. He shut his eyes tight and waited. There was a massive roar and a ripping, smashing sound. Heat from the blast scorched his face. A horrible burning smell filled his nostrils, making him choke. Slowly, Joe opened his eyes.

The plane had crashed metres from where he lay. It must have blown up on impact because there was hardly anything left but a charred, smoking wreck. The gravestone had saved his life, shielding his body from the full force of the explosion. Only the plane's tail had survived intact. Joe's blood turned cold when he glimpsed the sign on the tail. It was a black cross
– the symbol of the German Luftwaffe in the Second World War.

With a shaking hand, he reached through the long grass for the smartphone that had slipped from his grasp when he'd fallen. He prayed it wasn't broken.

The screen lit up. Thank goodness!

Nervously, he touched the "Timeshift" icon, scanned the screen and then touched "Emergency return".

* * *

The scene changed immediately. He was still lying there in the churchyard, but the wreck of the plane had disappeared. It was now a peaceful, sunny day. The only smell was fresh-mown grass, and the only sound was birdsong. Everything, in fact, was exactly as it ought to be.

A wave of relief washed through him. Had he dreamed the whole thing? It hadn't felt like a dream. And his face still felt tender from the burning heat.

"Joe! Where are you?"

He looked up to see his cousin Maya walking along the path towards the churchyard. Joe climbed gingerly to his feet.

"Hey, cuz!" she cried when she saw him. "I've been looking all over for you. What are you doing here? And what's happened to your face?"

Joe touched his sore cheek. His finger came away covered in soot. He hesitated, unsure what to say. He didn't know his cousin that well. He felt sure she'd laugh at him if he started telling her he'd just been back in time to the Battle of Britain. After all, she'd spent most of the past three days laughing at him for his strange country ways. That was when she wasn't completely ignoring him.

Joe had been sent to stay with Maya and her dad, Uncle Theo, here in Slade Common in south-east London. His parents thought it would do him good to spend some time with his relatives, instead of idling away his summer holiday reading detective stories at home in Dorset.

"It'll be fun!" his mum had assured him. "Your Uncle Theo's a historian, and you like history, don't you, Joe?"

That much was true. Uncle Theo *was* a historian, and Joe *did* like history. But what his mum hadn't told him was that Uncle Theo would be so busy writing his history books that he'd have hardly any time for Joe.

That meant Joe was forced to spend all his time with Maya.

She was Joe's age, but about as different from him as it was possible to be. Where Joe was quiet and polite, she was loud and rude. And she was *always* on the phone or texting her friends. She had about a hundred thousand of them, or so it seemed.

Joe could count his own friends on the fingers of one hand. He preferred books to people, if he was honest. And the books he loved most were detective stories. He'd read so many, he reckoned he could solve any crime. One day he'd be a famous detective. All he needed was a mystery to make his name – a mystery worthy of his talents.

As for Maya, he doubted she had time for mysteries. All she ever read were her friends' text messages.

She'd been on the phone just now in fact. She and Joe had been walking along the high street when Sarah (or was it Serena or Samantha or Susannah?) had called her. Bored with waiting for the conversation to end, Joe had wandered into the churchyard. He'd been standing by an overgrown grave when he'd spotted it, in the undergrowth at the foot of the gravestone – a smartphone. Joe had picked it up. The phone was bound to have the owner's details somewhere in it. He could return it to the owner himself – and perhaps get a reward.

So imagine his surprise when he'd switched it on and read this:

Hello Joe Smallwood.
Which time would you like to visit?

Joe had been struck dumb. How could a phone he'd just found possibly know his name? He'd never been to this place before. At least the question had seemed innocent enough – at first. Joe had assumed it would take him to a history website.

Beneath the question were some wheels that you could spin with your fingers: one wheel for the date, one for the month and one for the year. He'd spun the wheels to 18th August 1940, expecting to be given some facts about what had happened on that date in history. Next thing he knew, a loud drone was filling his ears and a German warplane was hurtling through the sky towards him!

The phone had actually sent him back in time.

If you would like to order this book, visit the ReadZone website: www.readzonebooks.com

FICTI⬤N EXPRESS

The Time Detectives:
The Mystery of Maddie Musgrove
by Alex Woolf

When Joe Smallwood goes to stay with his Uncle Theo
and cousin Maya life seems dull, until he finds a strange
smartphone nestling beside a gravestone. The phone
enables Joe and Maya to become time-travelling detectives
and takes them on an exciting adventure back to Victorian
times. Can they prove maidservant Maddie Musgrove's
innocence? Can they save her from the gallows?

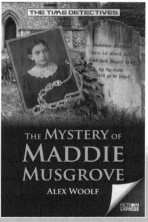

ISBN 978-1-783-22459-3

FICTI●N EXPRESS

The Time Detectives:
The Disappearance of Danny Doyle
by Alex Woolf

When the Time Detectives, Joe and Maya, stumble upon an old house in the middle of a wood, its occupant has a sad tale to tell. Michael was evacuated to Dorset during World War II with his twin brother, Danny. While there, Danny mysteriously disappeared and was never heard from again. Can Joe and Maya succeed where the police failed, journey back to 1941 and trace Michael's missing brother?

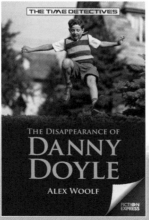

THE TIME DETECTIVES

THE DISAPPEARANCE OF
DANNY DOYLE
ALEX WOOLF

FICTI●N EXPRESS

ISBN 978-1-783-22458-6

The School for Supervillains
by Louie Stowell

Mandrake DeVille is heading to St Luthor's School for Supervillains, where a single act of kindness lands you in the detention pit, and only lying, cheating bullies get top marks. On paper, Mandrake's a model student: her parents are billionaire

ISBN 978-1-783-22460-9

supervillains, and she has superpowers. The trouble is, Mandrake secretly wants to save the world, not destroy it.

Drama Club
by Marie-Louise Jensen

Zoe and her friends are looking forward to a fun summer at Footlights – their local youth drama club. When their leader, the charismatic Mr Beaven, announces he wants to put on a major production at the end of the holidays, the whole cast is

ISBN 978-1-783-22457-9

very excited. Amidst rivalry, hopes, disappointments and disasters, will there be more drama on or off the stage?

About the Author

Sharon Gosling always wanted to be a writer. She started as an entertainment journalist, writing about television series such as *Stargate* and *Battlestar Galactica*. Her first novel was published under a pen name in 2010.

Sharon and her husband live in a very small cottage in a very remote village in the north of England, surrounded by sheep-dotted fells. The village has its own vampire, although Sharon hasn't met it yet. The cat might have, but he seems to have been sworn to secrecy and won't say a thing.

Sharon's e-books for Fiction Express include *The Ghosts of Eden Valley*, about a boy who moves from inner-city London to the wilds of Cumbria and sees strange ghost-like figures on the moors, *Shadow People*, a sci-fi adventure and *Threads*, the story of a young Victorian mill worker who tries to save the mill from sabotage.